Disney
CLUB PENGUIN
SHADOW GUY AND GAMMA GAL
HEROES UNITE
GG

GROSSET & DUNLAP
Published by the Penguin Group
Penguin Group (USA) Inc., 375 Hudson Street, New York, New York 10014, USA
Penguin Group (Canada), 90 Eglinton Avenue East, Suite 700, Toronto,
Ontario M4P 2Y3, Canada
(a division of Pearson Penguin Canada Inc.)
Penguin Books Ltd., 80 Strand, London WC2R 0RL, England
Penguin Group Ireland, 25 St. Stephen's Green, Dublin 2, Ireland
(a division of Penguin Books Ltd.)
Penguin Group (Australia), 250 Camberwell Road,
Camberwell, Victoria 3124, Australia
(a division of Pearson Australia Group Pty. Ltd.)
Penguin Books India Pvt. Ltd., 11 Community Centre, Panchsheel Park,
New Delhi–110 017, India
Penguin Group (NZ), 67 Apollo Drive, Rosedale, North Shore 0632, New Zealand
(a division of Pearson New Zealand Ltd.)
Penguin Books (South Africa) (Pty.) Ltd., 24 Sturdee Avenue,
Rosebank, Johannesburg 2196, South Africa

Penguin Books Ltd., Registered Offices: 80 Strand, London WC2R 0RL, England

Library of Congress Control Number: 2009032074

ISBN 978-0-448-45092-6 10 9 8 7 6 5 4 3

SHADOW GUY AND GAMMA GAL

HEROES UNITE

by Arie Kaplan
illustrated by Richard Carbajal

Grosset & Dunlap
An Imprint of Penguin Group (USA) Inc.

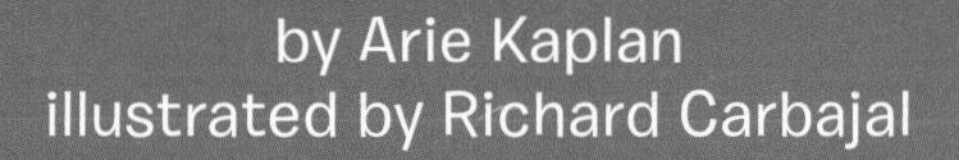

SUPERHEROES
TATE
ZEUS
Hi there! My name's Joe. Today, I'm doing my favorite thing. I'm drawing comic books, and the comic book I'm working on right now is called . . .
. . . Shadow Guy and Gamma Gal: Heroes Unite!
I'm still working on the first page.
All the others are blank!
Of course, I'll soon change that.
In fact, why don't you join me as I complete the rest of the pages?

My story stars the two superheroes from the Stage play *Squidzoid vs. Shadow Guy and Gamma Gal*. Do you remember them? Well, I always wondered how they met, so I made up this story. And I'm going to show it to you.

NIGHTCLUB

GIFT SHOP

Now, the first thing you have to know is that it all happened on this island . . .

. . . the island known as CLUB PENGUIN!

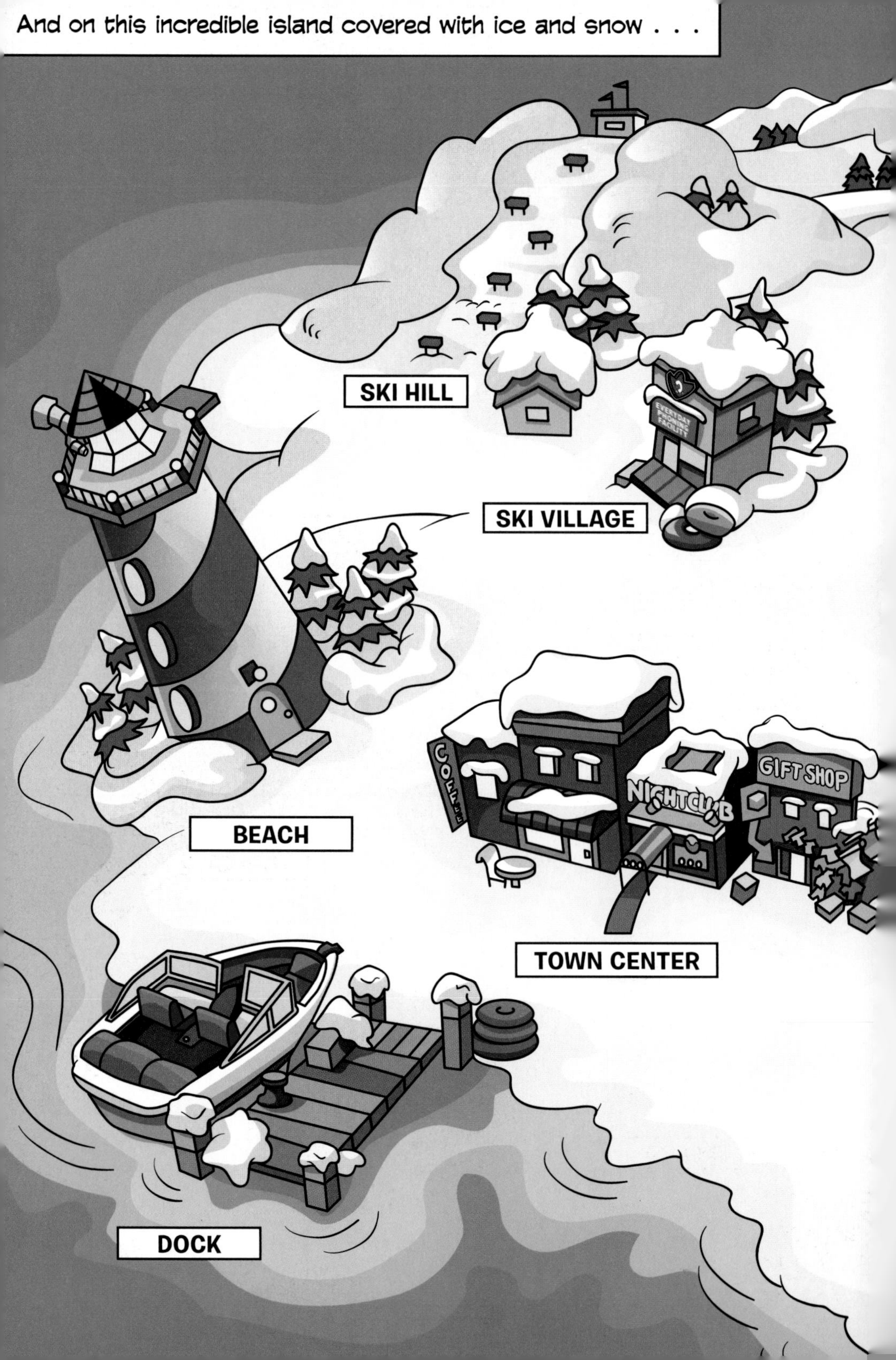
And on this incredible island covered with ice and snow . . .
SKI HILL
SKI VILLAGE
BEACH
COFFEE
NIGHTCLUB
GIFT SHOP
TOWN CENTER
DOCK

DOJO
ICEBERG
MINE
ICE RINK
COVE
SNOW FORTS
FOREST
PET SHOP
STAGE
PIZZA
PLAZA
MEMBER IGLOOS

. . . there lived a girl named Amy! Amy was fearless.
RIDGE RUN
YAHOOOOO!

And it was that fearlessness that led to her greatest adventure!
REEEEE!
WOW, WHAT'S THAT GLOWING THING?

WHOA! IT'S . . .
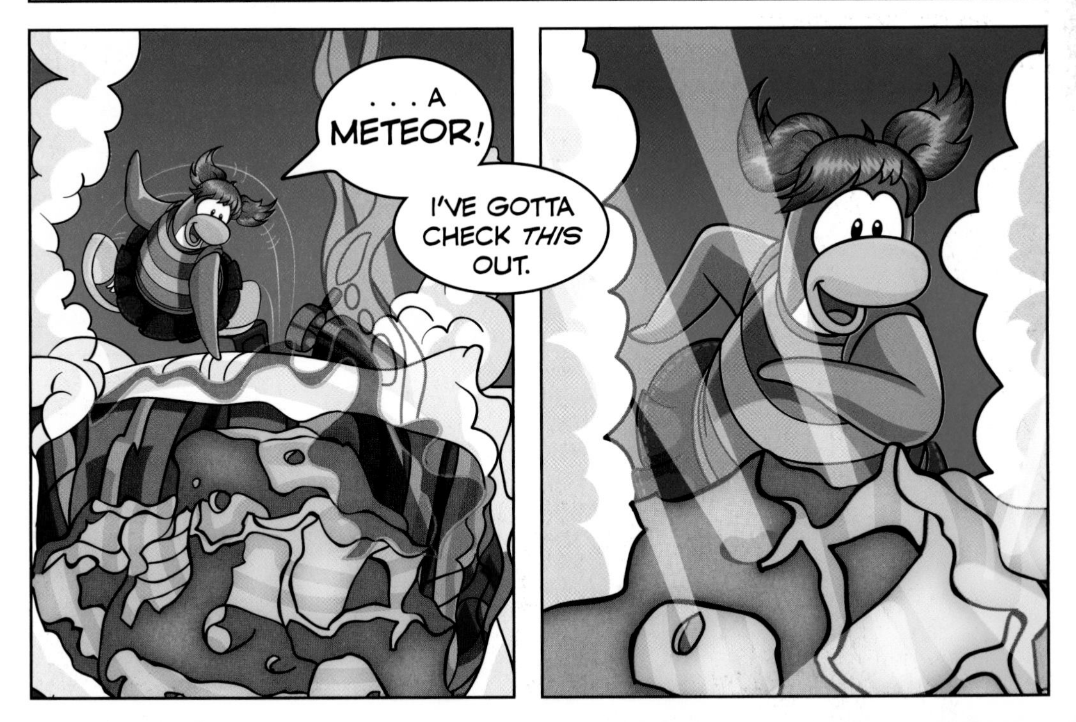
. . . A METEOR!
I'VE GOTTA CHECK *THIS* OUT.

HMM. I PROBABLY SHOULDN'T TOUCH THIS METEOR. I DON'T KNOW WHERE IT CAME FROM. BUT ON THE OTHER HAND . . .
. . . IT'S SO COOL!
I'LL JUST TOUCH IT FOR A SECOND. WHAT HARM CAN THAT DO?
MAYBE I SPOKE TOO SOON . . .

HA-HA! THIS TICKLES!
WOW!
YAWN! I THINK THAT METEOR MADE ME SLEEPY.

YAWN! GUESS I'LL JUST STOP AND TAKE A NAP.
SHOOP!
ZZZZZZZZZZZzz...

Later, inside the Dojo . . .
SENSEI? HOW DID I GET HERE?
AH, YOU'RE AWAKE.
WELCOME TO THE DOJO, YOUNG GRASSHOPPER!
I FOUND YOU OUTSIDE, SLEEPING. YOU LOOKED SERENE, LIKE THE PEACEFUL GOLDFISH.
I HAD THE WEIRDEST DREAM, SENSEI. I DREAMED THAT THIS METEOR ZAPPED ME . . .

. . . AND SUDDENLY I WAS GLOWING!
ZAPPPP!
WOW, DID YOU SEE WHAT I JUST DID, SENSEI? I ZAPPED THAT CHAIR!
GUESS IT WASN'T A DREAM.
IN YOUR HEART OF HEARTS THE METEOR IGNITED ONE GLOWING EMBER.
THE *METEOR*? IS THAT WHAT CAUSED THIS?
INDEED. THAT GLOWING ROCK MUST HAVE GIVEN YOU GAMMA POWERS.
I WONDER *WHAT ELSE* I CAN DO?
LIKE THE WISE DOLPHIN, I WILL TEACH YOU THE NINJA SKILLS NECESSARY TO HELP YOU UNDERSTAND YOUR POWERS.

WHEN CAN I START THE TRAINING?
WHY, AMY . . .
. . . ALL YOU HAD TO DO WAS ASK!
SO, WE KNOW THAT YOU CAN GLOW. LET'S SEE WHAT ELSE YOU CAN DO.
WELL, IT LOOKS LIKE I CAN FLY.
AND I CAN CREATE LIGHT.
LIKE THE ANCIENT TORTOISE, YOU ARE COMING OUT OF YOUR SHELL.

OOPS. SORRY, SENSEI.
LIKE THE SLEEPY SEA OTTER, I THINK WE SHALL CALL IT A DAY.
AMY, HEED MY WORDS. NOW THAT YOU HAVE THESE POWERS, PLEASE USE THEM FOR GOOD!
AS A SUPERHERO?
YES, BUT . . .
. . . YOU NEED MORE PRACTICE. TRAIN WITH ME IN SECRECY UNTIL YOU ARE DONE.

Meanwhile, Sam, a reporter for The Club Penguin Times, was interviewing Gary the Gadget Guy in his lab.
TRY IT!
ON
OUT OF ORDER
SO, GARY, CAN YOU TELL THE CLUB PENGUIN TIMES ABOUT YOUR LATEST GADGET?
ABSOLUTELY, SAM. AS AN INVENTOR, MY JOB IS TO COME UP WITH GADGETS THAT MAKE PENGUINS' LIVES EASIER. SO I'VE CREATED . . .
FILM
. . . THE TOASTER 3000. THIS WILL BE THE TOASTER OF THE FUTURE!

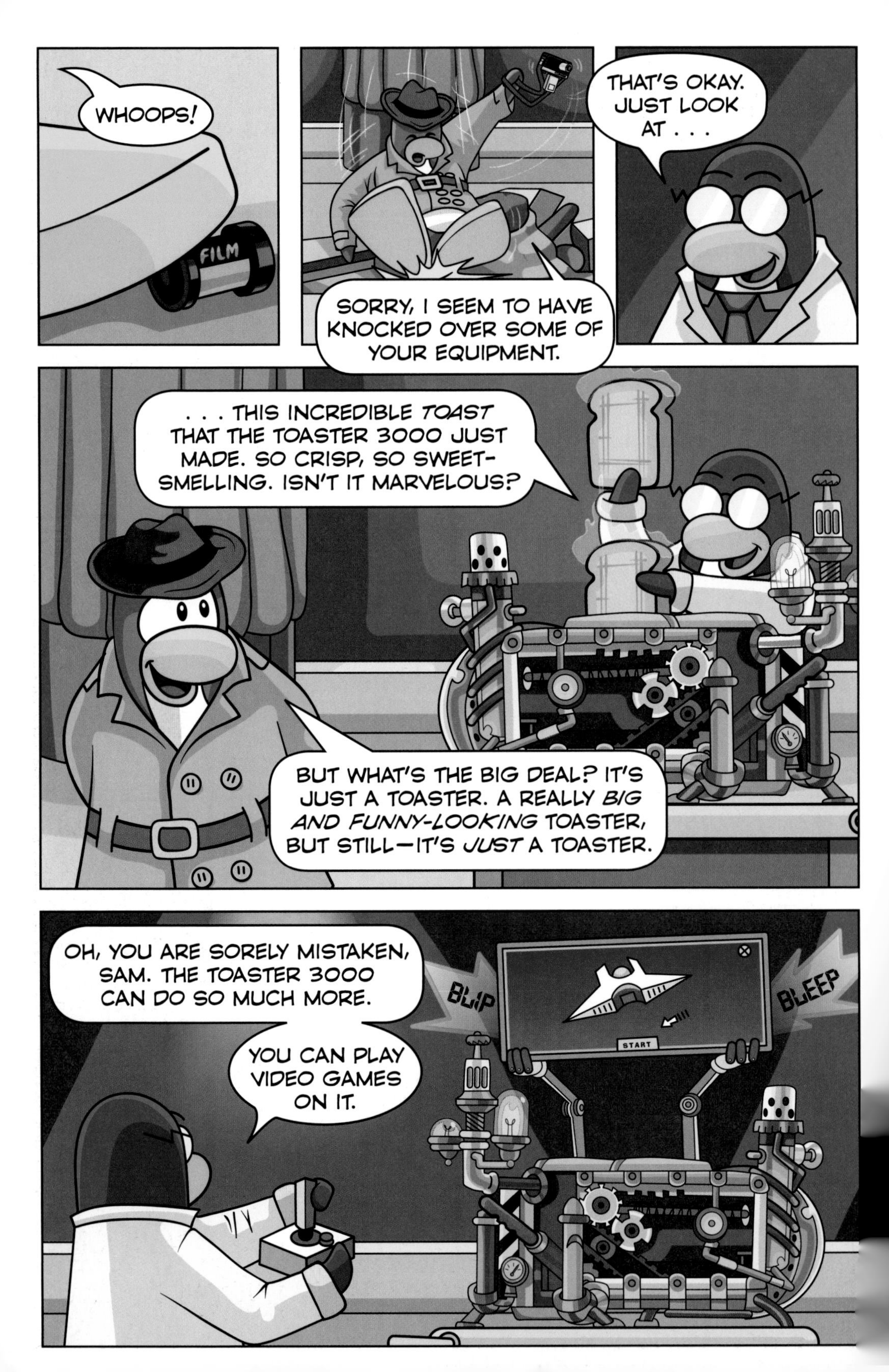
WHOOPS!
FILM
THAT'S OKAY. JUST LOOK AT . . .
SORRY, I SEEM TO HAVE KNOCKED OVER SOME OF YOUR EQUIPMENT.
. . . THIS INCREDIBLE *TOAST* THAT THE TOASTER 3000 JUST MADE. SO CRISP, SO SWEET-SMELLING. ISN'T IT MARVELOUS?
BUT WHAT'S THE BIG DEAL? IT'S JUST A TOASTER. A REALLY *BIG AND FUNNY-LOOKING* TOASTER, BUT STILL—IT'S *JUST* A TOASTER.
OH, YOU ARE SORELY MISTAKEN, SAM. THE TOASTER 3000 CAN DO SO MUCH MORE.
YOU CAN PLAY VIDEO GAMES ON IT.
BLIP
BLEEP
START

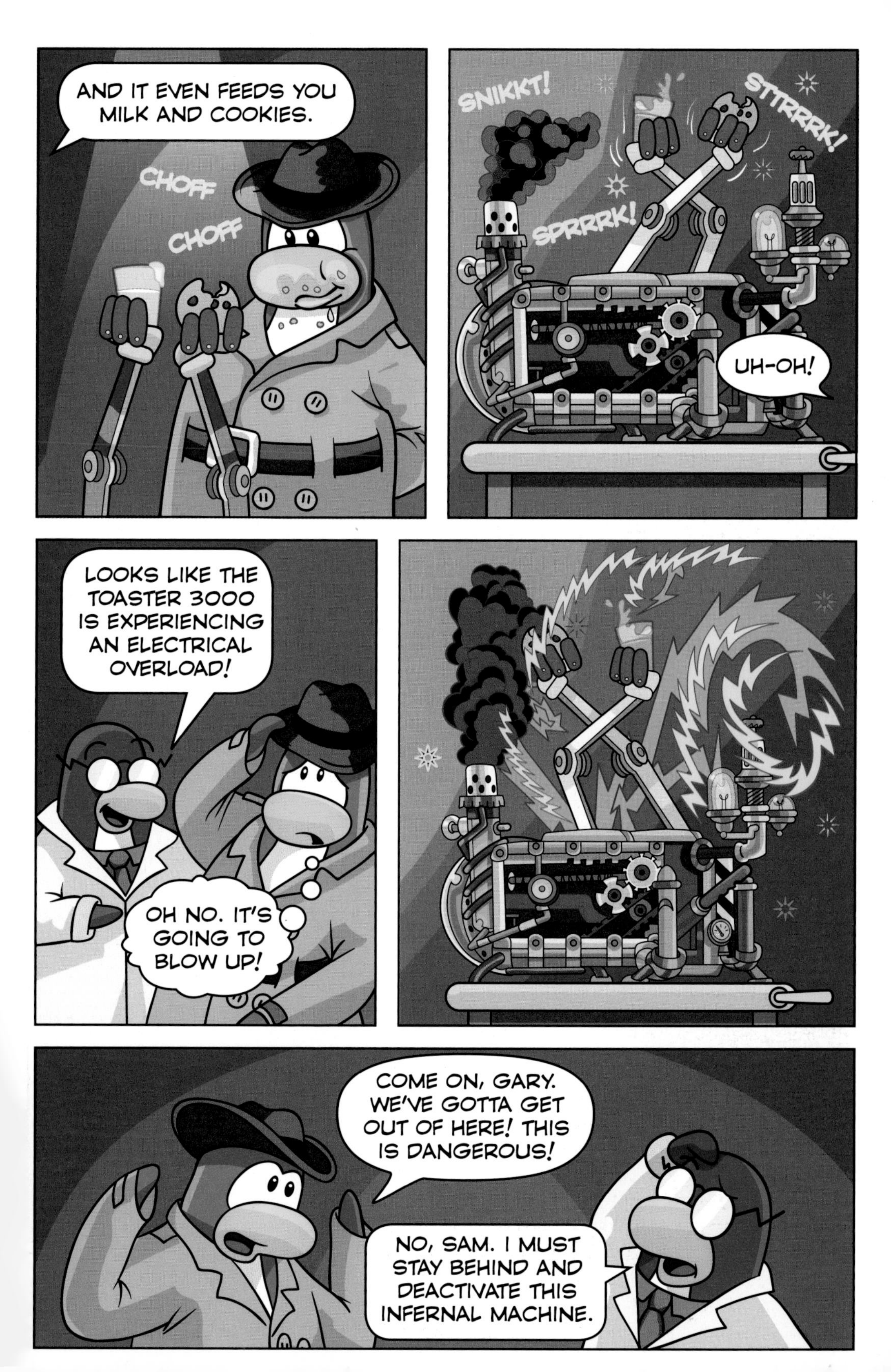
AND IT EVEN FEEDS YOU MILK AND COOKIES.
CHOFF
CHOFF
SNIKKT!
STTRRRK!
SPRRRK!
UH-OH!
LOOKS LIKE THE TOASTER 3000 IS EXPERIENCING AN ELECTRICAL OVERLOAD!
OH NO. IT'S GOING TO BLOW UP!
COME ON, GARY. WE'VE GOTTA GET OUT OF HERE! THIS IS DANGEROUS!
NO, SAM. I MUST STAY BEHIND AND DEACTIVATE THIS INFERNAL MACHINE.

I'VE GOTTA GET GARY OUT OF THE WAY BEFORE IT'S TOO LATE.
SAM! WHAT ARE YOU DOING?
COME ON, GARY, THIS IS NO TIME TO BE A HERO! WE JUST HAVE TO GET TO THE DOOR, AND THEN WE'LL BE SAFE!

OH NO. SAM!
ZZAAAPPP
YIKES! THAT'S COLD!

ARE YOU OKAY?
WELL, *THAT* DOESN'T HAPPEN EVERY DAY.
YEAH. CAN'T SAY THE SAME FOR THE TOASTER 3000, THOUGH.

BUT THERE'S STILL ONE THING I DON'T UNDERSTAND.
KLANG-G-LANG!
YOU WERE ZAPPED BY THE TOASTER 3000, AND YOU'RE *COMPLETELY UNHARMED.*
YEAH. IT JUST FELT . . . TINGLY.
I FEEL FINE NOW.
KAPOP!
SAM! WATCH OUT FOR THE DOOR!
WHOA! I'VE BECOME A *SHADOW*. HOW DID *THAT* HAPPEN?
THUNK!
OH MY!

HMM. YOU SEEM TO HAVE ABSORBED SOME ULTRAVIOLET LIGHT SPECTROMETERS.
TO PUT IT SIMPLY, THE TOASTER ZAPPED YOU AND IT . . . CHANGED YOU SOMEHOW!
YOU'RE NOT KIDDING. THIS IS COOL.
I WONDER WHAT ELSE YOU CAN DO.
GUESS THERE'S ONLY ONE WAY TO FIND OUT.
LOOK! I CAN CREEP ALONG THE WALL . . .
. . . OR ANY FLAT SURFACE. LIKE THIS WORKBENCH.
JUST LIKE A REAL SHADOW!
EXACTLY.

HMM . . .
LOOK WHAT I'M DOING. I CAN GRAB YOUR SHADOW!
EXTRAORDINARY! YOU'RE REMOVING MY SHADOW LIKE IT WAS A MERE OBJECT.
AND THAT'S NOT ALL. I HAVE AN IDEA.
HEY, YOU'RE ADDING MY SHADOW TO YOUR OWN. BUT WHY?
YOU'LL SEE!
INTERESTING! WITH MY SHADOW ADDED TO YOUR OWN SHADOW-SELF, YOU'RE BECOMING . . .

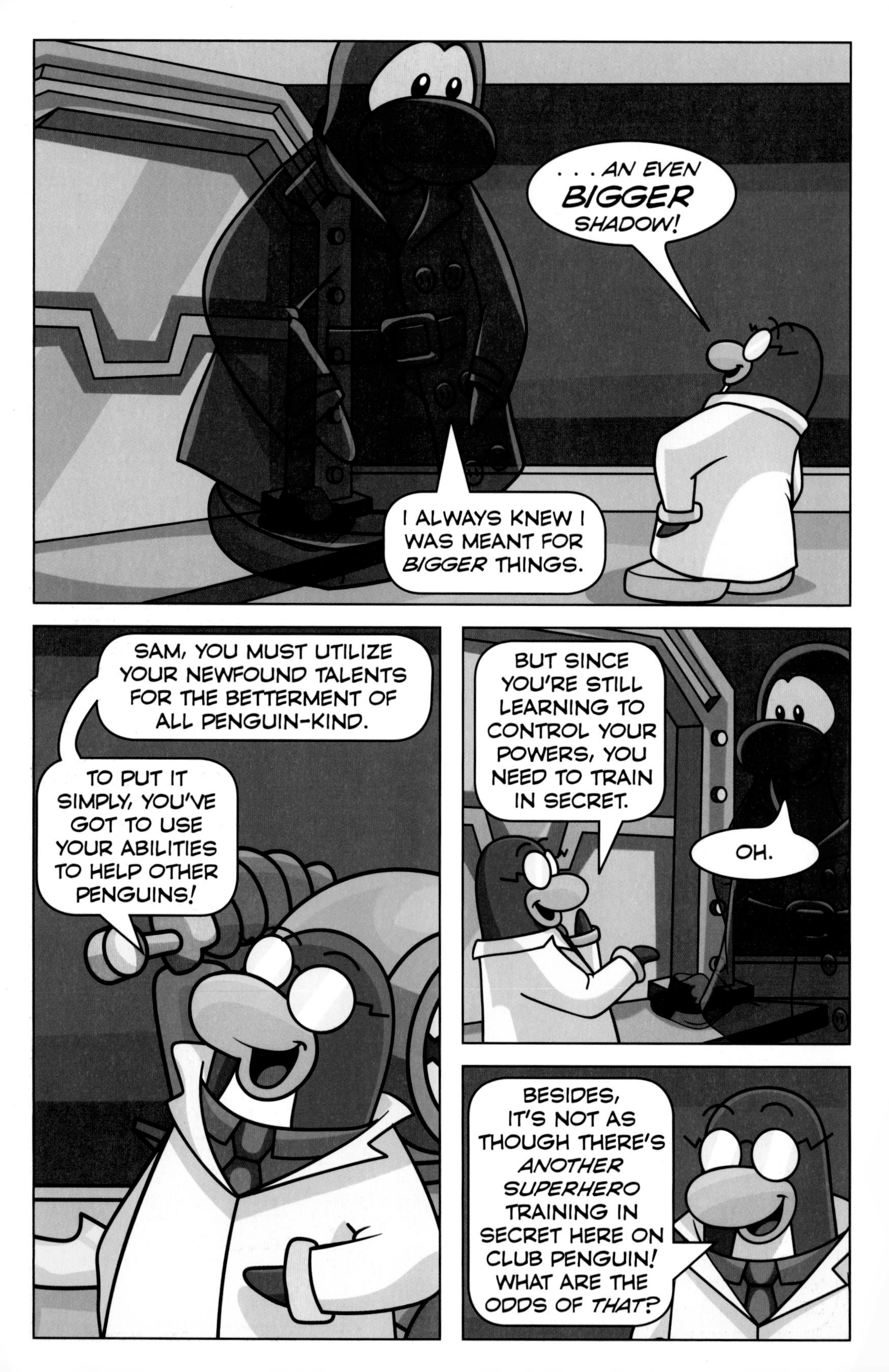

. . . AN EVEN *BIGGER* SHADOW!
I ALWAYS KNEW I WAS MEANT FOR *BIGGER* THINGS.
SAM, YOU MUST UTILIZE YOUR NEWFOUND TALENTS FOR THE BETTERMENT OF ALL PENGUIN-KIND.
TO PUT IT SIMPLY, YOU'VE GOT TO USE YOUR ABILITIES TO HELP OTHER PENGUINS!
BUT SINCE YOU'RE STILL LEARNING TO CONTROL YOUR POWERS, YOU NEED TO TRAIN IN SECRET.
OH.
BESIDES, IT'S NOT AS THOUGH THERE'S *ANOTHER SUPERHERO* TRAINING IN SECRET HERE ON CLUB PENGUIN! WHAT ARE THE ODDS OF *THAT*?

The very next day, Sam stopped by the Pizza Parlor to grab lunch . . .
KITCHEN
FISH DISH
COULD I PLEASE HAVE A PIECE OF SQUID AND SEAWEED PIZZA, WITH EXTRA HOT SAUCE?
COMIN' RIGHT UP! LEMME JUST GO TO THE KITCHEN. I GOT THIS NEW PIZZA DOUGH RECIPE THAT I'M REALLY EXCITED ABOUT!
DOO-DEE-DOO! GONNA MIX UP A BATCH OF DELICIOUS DOUGH, DON'T YA KNOW, MIX IT UP, TO AND FRO.
DOO-DEE-DOO! GONNA MAKE A DEEP DISH, IT'LL BE SO DEE-LISH, ANCHOVY IS MY FAVORITE FISH!

OH, MY CUSTOMERS WILL JUST LOVE THIS NEW PIZZA DOUGH RECIPE—
HEY, WHAT'S GOING ON? IT'S LIKE MY PIZZA DOUGH HAS COME TO LIFE!
BONK!
BONK!
BONK!
I CAN'T JUST SIT HERE WHILE THAT PIZZA DOUGH BLOB HOPS ALL OVER CLUB PENGUIN. BUT WHAT COULD I DO ABOUT IT?

AAAH!
HELP! MY PIZZA DOUGH HAS GONE CRAZY. SOMEONE'S GOTTA STOP IT!
GASP!
GULP!
HEY, WAIT A MINUTE! I'VE GOT SHADOW POWERS NOW! ALL RIGHT. THIS IS NO TIME TO BE AFRAID. I'VE GOT TO HELP MY FELLOW PENGUINS.
SPECIFICALLY, I'VE GOTTA GO INTO . . .
SHADOW MODE!
NOW, WHERE IS THAT PIZZA DOUGH BLOB?

THE STAGE
NOW SHOWING
LIVE
TWELFTH FISH
POETRY IN OCEAN
COME AND SEE!
TICKETS
PIZZA

THOU VILE LIVING SHADOW. WHAT ART THOU DOING?
HARK! YON SHADOW CREATURE APPEARS TO BE STEALING *OUR* SHADOWS!
TO BE OR NOT TO BE— A *SHADOW*!
SORRY, GUYS. I JUST NEED TO BORROW THESE FOR A MINUTE!
TRUST ME, FOLKS. YOU'LL THANK ME LATER.
HARRUMPH! I SHALL BELIEVE *THAT* WHEN I SEE IT.
I SEE IT. BUT I *DON'T* BELIEVE IT!
BELIEVE IT, FOLKS.
NOW IT'S TIME FOR A SNACK!

PET SHOP

WHOOSH
MUNCH
CRUNCH
MMM! THIS IS GOOD PIZZA DOUGH.
CHEW!

I CAN'T BELIEVE I ATE THE WHOLE THING.
URP!
EXCUSE ME.

TIME TO GO BACK TO MY NORMAL SIZE.
OOPS, LOOKS LIKE AUNT ARCTIC'S TAKING SOME PICTURES FOR THE PAPER. BETTER SLIP . . .
. . . AWAY!
And the very next day . . .
CLUB PENGUIN TIMES
Free Club Penguin Newspaper - Delivered every Thursday
WE NEED YOU!
IN FOCUS: PIZZATRON 3000
PAGE B1
ASK AUNT
NEW PLAY
THE STAGE!
MYSTERIOUS SHADOW GUY
SAVES CLUB PENGUIN!
BY AUNT ARCTIC
INSIDE
In Focus
Aunt Arctic
Top Secrets
Jokes & Riddles
Art & Comics
Poetry
Puzzles
Events

Meanwhile, on the other end of Club Penguin . . .

. . . a tree began to fall over.
RRRRUUUUUMMMBBBLLLEE

When it landed, it shook up everything in the Forest, frightening all the wild puffles!
SHLOOOOMPF

It caused a puffle stampede!
NIGHT CLUB
DISCO
OH NO! THE PUFFLES ARE RUNNING AMOK!
NO KIDDING!

At that very moment, at the Night Club . . .
EXIT
DANCE CONTEST
SIGN UP!
COME ON, SENSEI, WHY DON'T YOU DANCE WITH ME?
I DO NOT CARE MUCH FOR DANCING. LIKE THE GREAT GIANT CLAM, I PREFER TO REMAIN IN ONE PLACE.
LOOK, SENSEI, ISN'T *THIS* A GOOD WAY TO PRACTICE USING MY POWERS?
ER, UM . . . GLOWING LIKE A *DISCO STROBE LIGHT* IS NOT EXACTLY WHAT I HAD IN MIND. YOU SHOULD BE USING YOUR ABILITIES TO *HELP* YOUR FELLOW PENGUINS.
HELP MY FELLOW PENGUINS? HOW?

HEY! THERE ARE WILD PUFFLES EVERYWHERE! WHAT'S GOING ON??
HELP, RESCUE SQUAD! SEND SOME PENGUINS DOWN HERE IMMEDIATELY! WE'VE GOT A PROBLEM!
I REALIZE YOU RESCUE SQUAD FOLKS ARE DOING ALL YOU CAN, BUT THESE WILD PUFFLES ARE EVERYWHERE!
I KNOW, BUT WE CAN ONLY ROUND UP SOME OF THE WILD PUFFLES.
YEAH, IT'S NOT LIKE WE'RE *SUPERHEROES*!

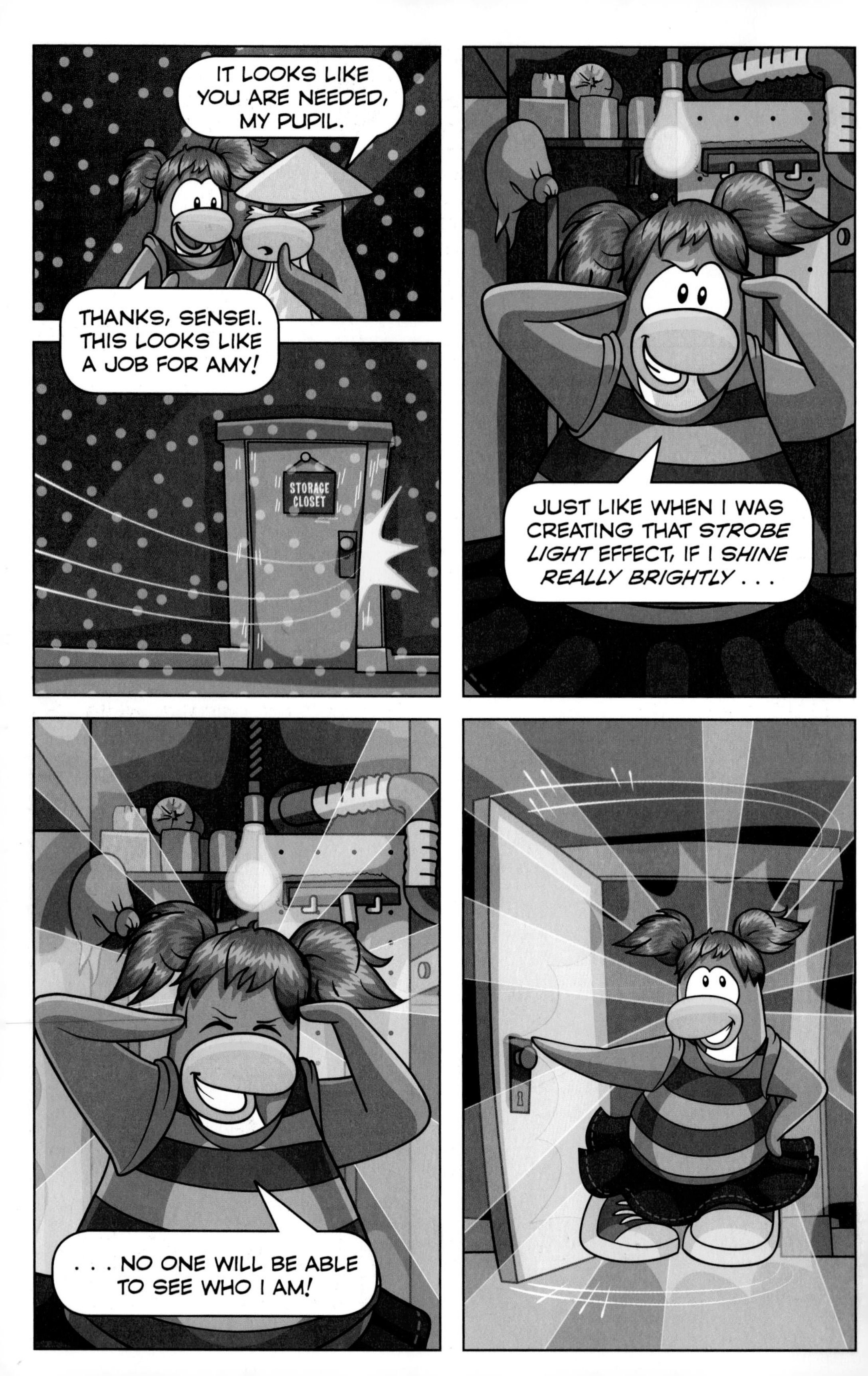
IT LOOKS LIKE YOU ARE NEEDED, MY PUPIL.
THANKS, SENSEI. THIS LOOKS LIKE A JOB FOR AMY!
STORAGE CLOSET
JUST LIKE WHEN I WAS CREATING THAT *STROBE LIGHT* EFFECT, IF I *SHINE REALLY BRIGHTLY* . . .
. . . NO ONE WILL BE ABLE TO SEE WHO I AM!

HI, PUFFLES!
IT'S WORKING. THEY'RE DISTRACTED BY MY GLOW! GUESS I ALWAYS WAS A PRETTY *BRIGHT* GAL!
THAT'S RIGHT, I'M LIKE THE PIED PIPER OF PUFFLES. FOLLOW ME, MY PUFFLE PALS . . .
EXIT
. . . INTO THE *PET SHOP*!
NOW ANY OF THE FOLKS ON CLUB PENGUIN CAN ADOPT THESE CUTE, LITTLE PUFFLES. THAT WAY, THEY WON'T RUN LOOSE. ISN'T THAT GREAT?
EXIT
IT SURE IS! ER, BUT I HAVE A QUESTION . . .
FOOD

. . . WHO ARE YOU?
WHO AM I? WELL . .
THAT'S A SECRET!

Moments later, back at the Dojo . . .
THE WAY YOU HANDLED THE WILD PUFFLE STAMPEDE SHOWS YOU ARE READY.
READY FOR WHAT?
LIKE THE HERMIT CRAB WHEN IT COMES OUT OF ITS SHELL, IT IS TIME FOR YOU TO REVEAL YOURSELF TO THE WORLD!
OH, SENSEI, I'VE BEEN THINKING THE VERY SAME THING. IN FACT . . .
THAT'S WHY I GOT THIS SUPERHERO COSTUME!
VERY IMPRESSIVE!
GG
FROM NOW ON, I'LL BE KNOWN AS . . .
. . . GAMMA GAL!
GG

Meanwhile, a similar conversation was happening over at Gary's lab.
SAM, YOU REALLY PROVED YOURSELF WITH YOUR TRIUMPH OVER THAT PIZZA DOUGH BLOB. WHICH IS WHY . . .
CPN
CLUB PENGUIN TI
NEW PLAY AT THE STAGE!
IN FOCUS: PIZZATRON 3000
MYSTERIOUS SHADOW GUY SAVES CLUB PENGUIN!
I SHOULD REVEAL MYSELF TO THE PUBLIC AS A SUPERHERO?
WELL, YES.
BUT WHAT WILL YOU CALL YOURSELF?
WELL, WITHOUT KNOWING IT WAS ME, AUNT ARCTIC CALLED ME "SHADOW GUY" IN THE NEWSPAPER. SO THAT'S WHAT I'LL CALL MYSELF: SHADOW GUY! NOW I JUST NEED TO FIND SOME PENGUINS WHO NEED SAVING.
CPN
Club Penguin News
THIS JUST IN! A GIANT SEA MONSTER IS STOMPING UP AND DOWN THE TOWN CENTER! THE RESCUE SQUAD AND EPF ARE OUT IN FULL FORCE, BUT IT SEEMS LIKE THIS SEA MONSTER CAN'T BE STOPPED!
TIME FOR SHADOW GUY TO SAVE THE DAY!
GOOD LUCK, SAM . . . ER, I MEAN, SHADOW GUY!

Shadow Guy zoomed toward the Town Center to stop the sea monster, not realizing Gamma Gal was up to the same thing.
OKAY, SEA MONSTER, COME AND GET—

HUH?
WHO ARE YOU?
I ASKED YOU FIRST!

I'M SHADOW GUY. I'M A SUPERHERO.
ME TOO!
I'M GAMMA GAL. I'M HERE TO STOP THE SEA MONSTER.
ME TOO!
GREAT TO MEET YOU, SHADOW GUY. NOW, IF YOU'LL EXCUSE ME, I'VE GOTTA GO FIGHT . . .

WAIT, WHAT DO YOU MEAN *YOU'VE* GOTTA GO FIGHT THE SEA MONSTER?
. . . THE SEA MONSTER!
GLABOOK! GLABOOK! MISH BLARR GLABOOK!
PET SHOP
THE STAGE
THE TWELFTH FISH
CLASSIC POETRY IN OCEAN
TICKETS
PIZZA

THE MORE TIME I WASTE, THE MORE DAMAGE THE SEA MONSTER WILL DO. I'VE GOT TO TRY TO STOP HIM!
B-BUT, DO YOU EVEN HAVE A PLAN?
DON'T WORRY. I KNOW WHAT TO DO!
I'LL DISTRACT THE SEA MONSTER WITH SOME BRIGHT, SHINY LIGHTS.
UH, MAYBE THAT ISN'T THE BEST IDEA.
WHY NOT? IT WORKED WITH SOME WILD PUFFLES I TAMED RECENTLY.
I DON'T KNOW. THIS SEA MONSTER'S MUCH BIGGER THAN A PUFFLE.
I'M DOING IT MY WAY AND THAT'S THAT!
BUT THAT'S DANGEROUS!
WELL, I'VE MADE UP MY MIND!
WHAT ARE YOU GOING TO DO, BARGE IN THERE AND TACKLE A GIANT SEA MONSTER WITH SOME *TWINKLY LIGHTS*?
SEE? I KNEW YOU'D UNDERSTAND. YOU'RE THE BEST!
BUT, BUT—I DIDN'T MEAN IT LIKE THAT!

LET'S SEE IF THE SEA MONSTER LIKES . . .
. . . THIS!
NIGHT CLUB
PET SHOP
NIGHT CLUB
PET SHOP
MISH BLARR GLABOOK!

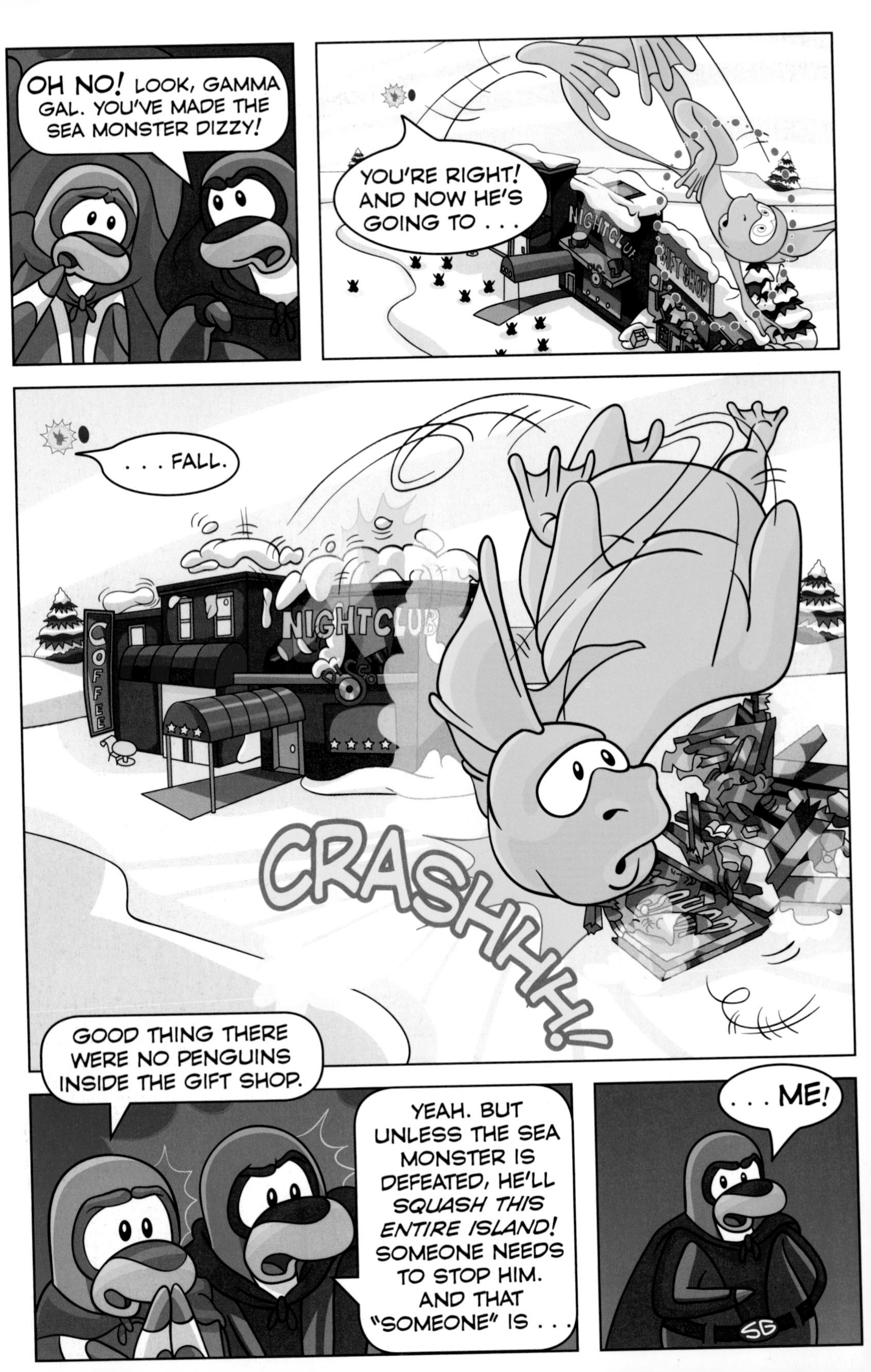
OH NO! LOOK, GAMMA GAL. YOU'VE MADE THE SEA MONSTER DIZZY!
YOU'RE RIGHT! AND NOW HE'S GOING TO . . .
NIGHTCLUB
GIFT SHOP
. . . FALL.
COFFEE
NIGHTCLUB
CRASHHH!
GOOD THING THERE WERE NO PENGUINS INSIDE THE GIFT SHOP.
YEAH. BUT UNLESS THE SEA MONSTER IS DEFEATED, HE'LL SQUASH THIS ENTIRE ISLAND! SOMEONE NEEDS TO STOP HIM. AND THAT "SOMEONE" IS . . .
. . . ME!
SG

KA-POP!

COME OVER HERE, YOU OVERGROWN SALMON!

HUH? MISH BLARR GLABOOK?
WHOOOAAA!
NIGHTCLUB
COFFEE

WHOOAA!
WELL, WELL, WELL . . .
GUESS WE BOTH STRUCK OUT, EH?
SO, NEITHER OF US HAS MANAGED TO STOP THE SEA MONSTER ALONE. WHAT DO WE DO NOW?

YOU KNOW, THAT MONSTER DOESN'T SEEM ANGRY OR EVEN UPSET.
GLABOOK?
HE JUST KEEPS SAYING "GLABOOK." WHAT IN THE WORLD IS GLABOOK?
HEY, THAT'S IT! WHY DON'T WE FIGURE OUT WHAT THIS "GLABOOK" *IS*! THEN WE CAN TAKE THE SEA MONSTER TO IT. THAT SHOULD MAKE HIM HAPPY. I DON'T THINK HE MEANS US ANY HARM.
WAIT A MINUTE, SHADOW GUY . . .

. . . YOU MEAN TO TELL ME THAT THE SEA MONSTER HAS NO IDEA THAT HE'S CAUSING ANY TROUBLE?
EXACTLY. I THINK HE'S JUST LOST, AND HE'S LOOKING FOR THIS "GLABOOK"!
NOW THAT WE KNOW THE SEA MONSTER ISN'T A BAD GUY, HOW WILL THAT HELP US STOP HIM?
SG
HMMM . . .
I'VE GOT IT!

WHEN EACH OF US WORKED ALONE, IT DIDN'T WORK.
THE SEA MONSTER IS SO BIG, WE'VE GOTTA JOIN FORCES *JUST TO GET HIS* ATTENTION!
SG
I HAVE AN IDEA. GAMMA GAL, CAN YOU CREATE SOME LIGHT?
YOU GOT IT!
NIGHTCLUB
SG

WHEN MY BALL OF LIGHT SHINES ON THE CITIZENS OF CLUB PENGUIN . . .
NIGHT CLUB
GLABOOK?
. . . IT MAKES THEIR SHADOWS APPEAR!
NIGHT CLUB
NOW, SHADOW GUY! DO YOUR THING!
OKAY! SO NOW I'LL . . .

. . . GO INTO SHADOW MODE . . .

. . . AND GRAB THE SHADOWS OF THE FOLKS IN THE CROWD . . .
YOINK!

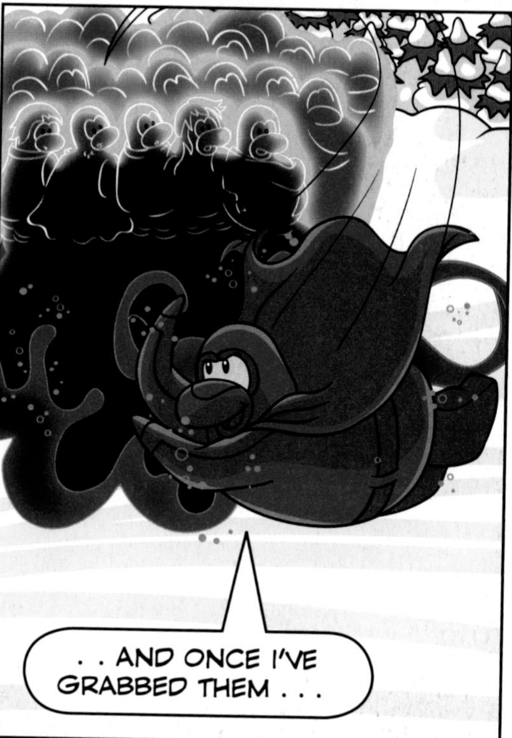
. . AND ONCE I'VE GRABBED THEM . . .

. . . I'LL ADD THEM TO *MY OWN* SHADOW-SELF!
IT'S THAT FLYING GUY AGAIN. NOW HE'S ADDING OUR SHADOWS TO HIS OWN!
WOW, THOSE SHADOWS ARE LIKE SPINACH. THEY'RE MAKING HIM *BIG AND STRONG!*

WOW! I'M ENORMOUS NOW. I'M ALMOST AS BIG AS THE SEA MONSTER!
NIGHT CLUB
HMM . . . YOU'RE STILL NOT BIG ENOUGH. NOW, GRAB THE *COFFEE SHOP'S SHADOW*, AND GRAB THE SHADOW FROM THE NIGHT CLUB . . .
. . . AND ADD *THOSE* SHADOWS TO YOU AS WELL!
NIGHTC
WOW! NOW I'M . . .

. . . EVEN BIGGER THAN THE SEA MONSTER!
I'M SORRY. I DON'T UNDERSTAND WHAT YOU'RE SAYING! I DON'T SPEAK SEA MONSTER LANGUAGE.
BLOY KOMPOJ KEKK KWAJWA GLABOOK?
NIGHTCLUB
SG

OHHH! I GET IT! YOU SPEAK PENGUIN. WELL, SO DO I!
YOU DO? WHY DIDN'T YOU SAY SO EARLIER?
NO ONE ASKED!

CAN YOU TAKE ME TO MY FRIEND GLABOOK?
OH, GLABOOK IS YOUR FRIEND. NOW I GET IT. WELL, DON'T WORRY.
THERE'S ONLY *ONE* PLACE ONE OF YOUR FRIENDS COULD BE!

FOLLOW ME!

WE'RE GOING TO THE
OCEAN, SEA MONSTER.
ONLY A FEW STEPS MORE!

HELLO? ARE THERE ANY SEA MONSTERS IN THE WATER? I'M LOOKING FOR GLABOOK.
DID SOMEONE CALL MY NAME?

GLABOOK?
IS THAT MY GOOD FRIEND WEBNARK?
I WAS WONDERING WHERE YOU HAD GONE OFF TO, WEBNARK!
I GOT LOST, GLABOOK. I TOOK A WRONG TURN GETTING SYRUP FOR MY SEAWEED PANCAKES.
THANK YOU FOR HELPING ME FIND MY FRIEND GLABOOK.
YOU'RE WELCOME.

SPLISH! SPLASH! SPLOSH!
WELL, I GUESS WE SAVED THE DAY.
YUP. AND WE DID IT TOGETHER!
KA-POP!
WE MAKE A GOOD TEAM!

I WONDER HOW EVERYONE ELSE IS DOING?

HELLO! I HOPE YOU DON'T MIND IF I INTERVIEW YOU FOR *THE CLUB PENGUIN TIMES*. WHAT WAS IT LIKE SAVING THE DAY FROM A FEARSOME SEA MONSTER?
UH, ACTUALLY, HE WASN'T FEARSOME.
THAT'S RIGHT. HE WAS JUST LOOKING FOR HIS FRIEND GLABOOK.
FASCINATING. SO DO YOU TWO SUPERHEROES HAVE NAMES?
YES. I'M SHADOW GUY, AND SHE'S GAMMA GAL.
BUT, SHADOW GUY, YOU FORGOT TO MENTION *THE MOST IMPORTANT PART* . . .
. . . WHICH IS THAT WE'RE A SUPERHERO **TEAM!**
WELL, GOODNESS, THAT *IS* A SCOOP! I GUESS I'LL ANNOUNCE IT TO MY READERS . . .

. . . WITH A *FRONT PAGE HEADLINE*, INTRODUCING THE TEAM OF SHADOW GUY AND GAMMA GAL, THE RESIDENT SUPERHEROES OF CLUB PENGUIN!
SHA-DOW-GUY! GAM-MA-GAL! SHA-DOW-GUY! GAM-MA-GAL!
NIGHT CLUB
YOU'VE ENACTED THE MOST SUPERB HEROIC FEATS EVER ACCOMPLISHED ON CLUB PENGUIN. OR, TO PUT IT MORE SIMPLY, HOORAY, SHADOW GUY!
LIKE THE BRAVE SHARK, YOU HAVE MADE QUITE A BIG SPLASH. I AM PROUD OF YOU, GAMMA GAL.

And just what was this new team of superheroes capable of?
NIGHT CLUB
You'll have to find out next time . . .
. . . in their next big adventure!
The End